WITHDRAWN

P9-AQM-352

A Happy Tale

A Happy Tale

Dorothy Butler • Pictures by John Hurford

Crocodile Books, USA

An imprint of Interlink Publishing Group, Inc.
NEW YORK

There was once a young woman called Mabel, who lived in a town on one side of a large island.

Unhappily, Mabel had no house to live in.

Happily, a friend named Charles, who lived in a town on the other side of the island, asked her to share his house with him.

Unhappily, the town was a long way away and Mabel had no money for the train fare.

Happily, a friend called Maud, who was learning to be a pilot, offered to take Mabel in her aeroplane.

Unhappily, Maud was not a very good pilot, and she tipped Mabel out in the middle of the island.

Happily, Mabel noticed a large, comfortable haystack in a field below, as she hurtled through the air.

Unhappily, there was a pitchfork in the haystack.

Happily, Mabel missed the pitchfork.

Unhappily, she missed the haystack.

Happily, Mabel landed in a pond.

Unhappily, she could not swim.

Happily, there was a farmer in the field.

Unhappily, the farmer could not swim either.

Happily, he managed to rescue Mabel with the pitchfork from the haystack.

Unhappily, the bull who lived in the field did not like all this fuss.

Happily, Mabel and the farmer managed to beat the bull to the fence and leap over.

Unhappily, they landed on a wasps' nest.

Happily, Mabel was rather stout, and she squashed the wasps' nest flat.

Unhappily, she also squashed the farmer flat.

Happily, the farmer and Mabel took a fancy to one another.

Unhappily, Mabel remembered that she was supposed to be joining Charles on the other side of the island.

Happily, Maud and Charles had taken a fancy to one another, so the story ended...

HAPPILY.

For Lyn Kriegler, from both of us
DB and JH

First American edition published 1990 by
Crocodile Books, USA
An imprint of Interlink Publishing Group, Inc.
99 Seventh Avenue • Brooklyn, New York 11215

Text © Dorothy Butler 1990
Illustrations © John Hurford 1990

Library of Congress Cataloging-in-Publication Data

Butler, Dorothy, 1925-
    A happy tale / Dorothy Butler : pictures by John Hurford.
  — 1st American ed.
        p.   cm.
    Summary: Both good and bad luck accompany Mabel as she
tries to get across her island to her new home.
    ISBN 0-940793-61-X
    [1. Luck — Fiction.] I. Hurford, John, ill, II. Title.
PZ7.B976Hap 1990
[Fic]—dc20   90-34500
                                                                  CIP
                                                                  AC

ISBN 0-940793-61-X

Printed and bound in Hong Kong